I0533840

SNOOPING CAN BE

Scary

*Books by Linda Hudson Hoagland
from Jan-Carol Publishing, Inc:*

LINDSAY HARRIS MURDER MYSTERY SERIES:
SNOOPING CAN BE SCARY
SNOOPING CAN BE DANGEROUS
SNOOPING CAN BE CONTAGIOUS
SNOOPING CAN BE DEVIOUS
SNOOPING CAN BE DOGGONE DEADLY
SNOOPING CAN BE HELPFUL–SOMETIMES
SNOOPING CAN BE UNCOMFORTABLE

THE BEST DARN SECRET
ONWARD & UPWARD
MISSING SAMMY

SNOOPING CAN BE

Scary

LINDA HUDSON HOAGLAND

Jan-Carol
Publishing, Inc
"every story needs a book"

Snooping Can Be Scary
Linda Hudson Hoagland

Published August 2018
Little Creek Books
Imprint of Jan-Carol Publishing, Inc.
All rights reserved
Copyright © 2018 by Linda Hudson Hoagland

This is a work of fiction. Any resemblance to actual persons, either living
or dead is entirely coincidental. All names, characters and events are the product
of the author's imagination.

This book may not be reproduced in whole or part, in any manner whatsoever
without written permission, with the exception of brief quotations within
book reviews or articles.

ISBN: 978-1-945619-71-7
Library of Congress Control Number: 2018954989

You may contact the publisher:
Jan-Carol Publishing, Inc.
PO Box 701
Johnson City, TN 37605
publisher@jancarolpublishing.com
jancarolpublishing.com

This Book Is Dedicated To My Sons:
Michael E. Hudson
Matthew A. Hudson

DEAR READER

Emily wants company when she goes to explore a haunted house. When she asks her mom, Lindsay, for permission along with her presence for the excursion, she is happy when her mom consents with one drawback. They will have to wait a couple of days until Lindsay can get some background information about the house in the woods.

Have the people who were murdered in that house remained after death to maintain their control over any future inhabitants?

When Emily goes missing, is she being held in that house? If so, why?

Lindsay and her amateur troop of sleuths find it necessary to look for the missing teenager. Lindsay, Ellen, Ryan, Jed, and Marnie start searching and run head long into more trouble than they ever expected.

This is the seventh volume of *A Lindsay Harris Murder Mystery Series* and it explores a world that might be filled with ghosts and haunted houses, proving that *SNOOPING CAN BE SCARY.*

ACKNOWLEDGMENTS

Janie C. Jessee, publisher of ten of my books, must be acknowledged for allowing me to do what I must do—write.

A special thanks to Tammy Robinson Smith for asking me to start this little series.

Chapter 1

M om, did you know there is a haunted house at the end of the street?" asked Emily, excited.

"No, what house would that be?" I asked skeptically.

"Mary told me you go to the end of our street, walk into the woods, and the house is hidden from the road behind the bushes and trees," said Emily.

"You haven't been there, have you?" I asked.

"Yeah, Ellen and I went with Mary to see the place in the daylight. We didn't see anything unusual but we really need to go back there at night," said Emily with a questioning tone.

"What are you trying to say, Em?"

"Can we all go exploring tonight and see if there are any ghosts in that house?" Emily asked in a pleading tone of voice.

"Ghosts? Do you believe in ghosts?" I asked.

"Of course, don't you?" asked Emily.

"Well, I'm just not sure. I haven't met one, have you?" I asked.

"No, no, I haven't. That's why I want to go to the haunted house. I want to see if they really exist," answered Emily.

"Oh, I see. You want to investigate like a detective might do. Is that right?" I asked.

"Yes, I want to write my semester essay about looking for the

1

ghost," said Emily with an encouraging smile.

"Was that your idea or your teacher's suggestion?" I asked.

"Mine, of course, Mrs. Smith wouldn't dare ask us to do anything like that, but I really want to do it, Mom."

"When do you want to do this investigation?" I asked. I seemed to be coming around to the idea for some strange reason.

"Tonight."

"I don't think so, not tonight. Actually, I want to think about this idea for a day or two. I want to do a little checking on my own. I will try to find out who really owns that property and what happened to them to cause the house to be haunted. That will take me a couple of days. I can do it while I'm at work. It's a good thing I work for a lawyer. I know what rocks to look under to find answers," I explained.

"Then we can go ghost hunting," said Emily not bothering to hide her excitement.

Chapter 2

"What have I gotten myself into?" I mumbled as I climbed into my car to drive to work. I really wasn't opposed to the idea of checking out the house at the end of the street. For that matter, I didn't know the house was there and I was curious.

On my way to work the next morning, I decided to locate the house in the woods.

The kids had already boarded the school bus, so I knew they wouldn't catch me doing exactly what I told them not to do.

I drove slowly to where I thought the street came to a dead end—at least, that was what the sign indicated. I gazed at a large stand of trees that loomed up before me when I exited my car. The trees were relatively close together, giving them a forbidding appearance. The branches crisscrossed so closely together that all the leaves had yet to fall to the ground. A dark canopy was overhead, preventing the morning sun from shining through.

My mind was playing tricks on me because, as I stared into the eerie darkness beneath the trees, a chill raced down my spine.

"Stop it, Linds," I scolded myself for being such a wimp.

I moved forward as if I were walking to face my judgement day. I held my eyes wide open, not allowing myself to blink.

"Get a grip," I said softly as I moved my gaze from side to side.

3

I truly didn't know what I was expecting to run into, but my mind was totally scared.

I forced my eyes to blink, I lowered my gaze to the ground, and I moved on following a path that had been worn by many footsteps in the distant past. I started to hum softly to combat the need to turn tail and run. The path appeared to grow wider, so I lifted my gaze from the ground and to see what was in front of me.

"Wow," I said as I saw before me what appeared to be a three-story house, and a wooden frame with large dormers protruding from the roof on the third floor. The paint was weathered and scaling, some of the windows were cracked but the pieces had not fallen to the ground, and the giant front door was slightly ajar.

Oh, how I wanted to walk inside to take a peek, but I knew I had to go to work and not get tangled up into a snooping event.

I walked across the front porch so I could stick my head inside to get a glimpse of the interior. I had to push on the heavy door a bit so it would open wide enough for me to hook my head around it.

FLASH!

The brightness was blinding. I jerked back from the door and fought to keep myself upright. As soon as I gained my composure, I started running to my car. I believe I screamed when the flash happened, but I wasn't quite sure if the sound came out of my mouth.

I reached my car, jumped in, and took off as fast as I could without killing myself and anyone else in my way.

"My God," I mumbled as I tried to get my nerves to refrain from tingling all over my body. "What in the world happened?"

I forced myself to slow my driving speed so I could get to work without earning a speeding ticket. I was going to be a few minutes late, but that was okay. Wayne was out of town and wouldn't be there to chastise me. For that, I was very grateful. I wasn't sure I could withstand the criticism and the lecture I would get about the fact that I should mind my own business.

4

Chapter 3

I parked my car and sat still for a few moments. I had to get my work face on before I walked through the office door. Thankfully, Annie had already arrived and had completed the opening up routine. That saved me a few precious moments for sitting at my desk and saying a short thank you for the One above.

"Are you all right, Lindsay?" asked Annie when I walked passed her desk.

"Yeah, sure, what makes you ask?" I said as nonchalantly as I could manage.

"You look a little flustered," Annie said with concern.

"Yes, I guess I am flustered," I said.

"Why? What happened?"

"You wouldn't believe me if I told you," I said.

"Aw come on, Linds. Tell me,"

"I went exploring around a haunted house this morning, and I managed to get scared to death," I said with a forced smile.

I went on to tell her what happened including the flash and the fact that I ran for my life. I added that my kids wanted to visit the same place at night.

"What do you think that flash was?" Annie asked.

"I don't know and I was too scared to find out."

5

"I bet it was probably a booby trap or surveillance camera of some kind," suggested Annie.

"Yes, it could have been that. All I know is it really scared me," I said.

"Are you going to let your kids explore?" Annie asked.

"I'm not sure. I need to do some more checking before I let them go near the place."

"How are you going to do that?" Annie asked.

"I'm going to the courthouse to ask Marnie to give me a hand," I answered.

I went to my office and glanced at the pile of files on my desk awaiting my attention. Because I do so many real estate files for Wayne, I knew no one would wonder about my checking on another piece of property.

It occurred to me that I didn't see an address written anywhere that would pinpoint the house on a street map. But it was at the dead end of my street, and that should help.

I grabbed a file folder and opened it so I would appear to be tackling the tasks inside. Then, I moved it off center of my desk, grabbed a notepad, and entered Marnie's work number into the phone.

"Marnie, can you look something up for me?" I asked in a whisper.

"What is it?" she asked loudly letting me know she could barely hear me.

"I forgot Wayne isn't here," I explained as I raised my voice to a normal range.

"Well, what is it?" Marnie asked.

"There is a big, three-story house at the end of my street. It's hidden behind a stand of trees, so I didn't even know it was there. Anyway, what I need is to find out who used to own it and why it is standing empty," I said.

"What's the name of your street?" Marnie asked.

6

"You know what it is. You've been to my house a million times," I said sarcastically.

"I know but I'm trying to appear professional," Marnie said in a whisper.

"Is the boss close by?" I asked.

"Yes, that is the case," Marnie said, trying to hide the fact that the call was personal.

"Will you do what I asked?" I said. I was hoping this conversation would save me a time-consuming trip to the courthouse.

"All right, but it might take me a day or two," said Marnie.

"That's fine. Are you going to be able to meet me for lunch today?" I asked.

"No, I've got to do something for my boss. Can we meet tomorrow?"

"Yes, that is fine with me. Give me a call later," I said as I tried to hide my disappointment. I hated to go to a restaurant to eat alone.

"Annie, where are you going for lunch today?" I shouted down the hallway.

"My usual, the hamburger joint down the street. Do you want me to pick up something for you?" she asked.

"Yep."

I turned my mind toward the work I had moved aside.

Chapter 4

On my way home from work, I was drawn to the house at the end of my street. I didn't want to visit it, I just wanted to drive passed it to see if anyone else was enticed to spend some time there.

I had to pass my own house where I glanced at the front windows to see that a light had been lit. That was my signal from the kids that they were all present and accounted for so I could breathe a sigh of relief before entering the house.

I slowed my car to a crawl. I really didn't know why I felt I had to slow down.

I saw flashes of something light colored through the trees. Of course, my mind flew to the absolutely impossible explanation.

"It's not ghosts," I mumbled as I tried to force my mind to think about what else the flashes of light colored images could be. I wanted to jump out of my car and go check on whatever it was.

"No—go home," I said loudly.

I turned my car around and headed for home.

"Hey mom, where did you go?" asked Ryan when I arrived.

"I drove down to the house your sisters want to check out," I answered truthfully.

"You mean the haunted one?" he asked.

8

"You know about that too? Why didn't you guys tell me about it being there before this?" I asked.

"We thought you knew about it. I t wasn't a secret, at least, I didn't think it was," Ryan said.

"Well, I didn't even know there was a house in those trees. Do you know anything about it?" I asked my seemingly informed son.

"The family, what was left of them, moved out long before we moved onto this street," he said.

"What do you mean 'what was left of them?'" I asked curiously.

"Most of them were murdered by some maniac. That's what I was told by some of my friends," Ryan said.

"Why did that maniac kill them?" I asked.

Before Ryan could answer, Emily entered the room.

"Em, tell mom about the killings in the house at the end of the street," urged Ryan.

"I don't know much about it," Emily said.

"You're the one who told me about the killings," snapped Ryan.

"I thought you wanted to check that house out because you just found out about it," I said accusingly.

"Okay, okay, I'll tell you what I heard from my classmates."

"And that is..." I prompted.

"There was some kind of love affair that went bad. The husband shot his wife and her lover in front of their kids," Emily explained.

"How old were the kids?" I asked.

"Young, one of them hadn't started school yet," Emily answered.

"What happened to the kids?" I asked.

"Nothing—they lived in the house until they grew up and moved away," said Emily.

"Who lived with them to take care of them?" I asked.

"They had a widowed aunt on the mother's side of the family

that moved in and stayed until she died unexpectedly. Someone said she was murdered, too. After that, the kids wanted out of that bad luck house. They were afraid they would be next," said Emily.

"How long has the house been empty?" I probed.

"Years, I don't know how many," answered Emily.

"Do you know the names of the people who lived there?" I asked.

"Johnson were the original couple. They actually built the house. I don't know the name of the lover or the aunt that raised the kids," said Emily.

"Who or what are you looking for when you got to the house to check it out?" I asked Emily.

"The ghosts of the lovers and the aunt. People have seen all three of them," she said excitedly.

"Why didn't you tell me all of this in the first place?" I demanded.

"I was afraid you wouldn't let me go," she said sheepishly.

"You might have been right about that," I agreed.

"Well, what about now?" Emily asked.

"I want to find out about that house and its inhabitants myself. So, you can go but I have to go with you. Deal?" I asked.

"Deal," said Emily as a smile appeared on her lips.

"It won't happen until I do some more checking. I have Marnie working on it. She will let me know as soon as she has time to dig into the records," I explained.

"Okay," said Emily as the smile disappeared from her lips.

"Where's your sister?" I asked Emily.

"In her room sulking," she said sarcastically.

"Why?"

"She can tell you," said Emily as she walked down the hallway towards her bedroom.

Chapter 5

I walked slowly down the hall to Ellen's room where I tapped on the door.

"Go away!" shouted Ellen.

"It's mom. Let me in," I said barely above a whisper.

"All right, come on in," she said softly.

"What's wrong, Ellen?"

"Nothing, I just want to be alone," she said sullenly.

"That doesn't sound like my Ellen. You are the happy go lucky person in this family. Now, what's got you all out of sorts?" I asked.

Suddenly the dam burst and the tears started flowing. I put my arms around her and let her cry. It had been a while since I'd had to endure the flood of tears caused by teenage angst.

"All right now, tell me what's wrong," I said softly as I straightened her hair a bit. Both of my daughters had driven me crazy with their long locks of hair hanging over their eyes.

"You'll just laugh at me," sniffled Ellen.

"No I won't, I promise," I said as I coaxed her to open up and tell me her problem.

"Well, there's a dance on Friday afternoon and I don't have a date," she said as the tears started to flow again.

"You aren't old enough to go out on a date," I said softly.

11

"I knew you would say that, but that's not the problem," she sniffled.

"What's the problem?" I asked as I tried to hide my confusion.

"No one asked me to go," she whimpered.

"Ellen, your guy friends probably know you can't go, so they don't ask. Don't you think that might be the reason?" I asked as I tried to soothe her jagged feelings.

"Oh, well maybe, but it would have been nice to be asked. Emily was asked and she said she is going," said Ellen with a scornful look of her face.

"Oh? Really? Who asked her to the dance?" I probed.

"He's a new guy in our school. He just moved into the house at the end of the street," she explained.

"You mean the house in the woods?" I asked.

"No, it's the last one before you get to the woods. It had been empty for a long time. There seemed to have been an ownership problem, but he said that finally got settled," Ellen said.

"What's his name, the new guy I mean?" I asked.

"Tim Riley."

"Now, you stop crying about not being asked to go to the dance. You know all of the local guys know you can't date yet. What kind of dance is it?" I said.

"It's a costume dance for Halloween. I think it's going to be a lot of fun and there should be a lot of crazy costumes at the dance," Ellen said.

"Can you go stag?" I asked.

"Stag? What's stag?" Ellen asked.

"No date, just go by yourself," I explained.

"I guess so."

"Then that's what you will do," I said encouragingly.

"What about Emily?"

"She will have to go stag. She will not be allowed to go with Tim Riley. I will drive both of you and pick you up after the dance," I said

12

sternly.

"Good," Ellen mumbled as I left her bedroom.

Emily was in the living room watching television so I decided to start up a conversation about the Friday afternoon plans.

"Em, who is Tim Riley?"

"She told you, didn't she?" Emily asked with a hint of anger in her voice.

"Ellen told me you had a date to go to the dance with Tim Riley. Do you?" I asked.

"No, I just told her that. I knew you wouldn't let me go," Emily said smugly.

I'm just going to meet him there. Is that okay?"

"You shouldn't lie to your sister," I said in a scolding tone.

"Okay, I won't do it anymore," said Emily in a tone that definitely was not sincere.

"I mean it, Em."

"I know, I know. When can we go investigate the house in the woods?" Emily asked.

"In a couple of days, I hope. I'm still doing some checking, or at least, Marnie is checking for me."

"Mom, Tim Riley told me that he used to live in that house when he was a little boy."

"Is that right?" I asked.

Emily knew how to change the subject and get me interested in what she wanted me to do.

"I'll run that name passed Marnie and see what she can come up with, but for now, the house investigation will have to wait."

"Halloween will be here soon. We need to get it done before then," said Emily.

"We've still got time. Why before Halloween?" I asked.

"That's when all the ghosts come out big time."

"Who told you that?" I asked.

"Everybody."

Chapter 6

I chased Emily out of the living room with the threat of no cell phone for a week if she didn't get ready for bed.

As soon as the room was quiet, the house telephone startled me into reality.

"Hello?" I said as I took attendance in my mind of who was present in my house.

"Linds, what's new?" asked the cheerful voice of Jed, the feature story writer for the newspaper in a city about fifty miles to the west of Stillwell.

"Hey, Jed, what's new with you?" I asked.

"Have you got any hot news stories for me?" he asked.

"No, it's been pretty quiet around here. That's a good thing, you know," I answered.

"It isn't good news for me because I have to come up with some ideas for future feature stories and not use the same old ideas over and over again."

"It's almost Halloween and we, the girls and I, are going to go ghost hunting. Do you want to ghost hunt with us?" I asked as a laugh escaped from my mouth.

"Ghost hunting? Are you serious?" he asked.

"Yes, it's Emily's idea but I won't let her go without me. Ryan

14

will probably go along just so his sisters won't think he is a wimp."

"I don't blame you for not letting the girls go alone. Anything can happen when you ghost hunt. You might even see one," he said without a bit of sincerity,

"Have you written a new story about ghost hunting this year?" I asked.

"Nope. When are you planning this hunting trip?" he asked.

"In a couple of days; say, how about the day after tomorrow?"

"I'll be there. I just need to know the time," Jed said.

"After dark, of course."

"Of course," he mumbled.

I picked up my crochet project to see if I could complete a couple of rows on my newest angel afghan pattern.

Before long I was asleep sitting on my favorite chair with the television making a soft drone of voices to cover any other disturbances from a creaking house.

***

Visions of ghosts were racing through my mind. Fog was rising from the ground and sounds of wind rustling the dry leaves on the trees assaulted my ears. "Em, stop! At least, slow down! Take your time," I shouted.

Emily paid no mind to me and kept forging ahead up the steps to the front porch of the old house. As she approached the front door, it swung open and a puff of breeze carried an awful smell out to us.

"What is that?" I asked Emily who was standing in front of me gagging from the odor.

"Something's dead in there," Em said once the gagging halted.

"Maybe we shouldn't go inside," I suggested as I tried to breathe through my mouth.

"Yes, we have to go inside. We have to find out what is causing that smell," said Emily a bit sterner than she should have.

15

We entered the house and saw nothing that would cause the horrible smell so we continued walking. We were in the foyer with rooms off to the left and right.

The room to the right was dark when we entered but the smell was horrific.

"Mom, look at that!" Emily screamed.

***

I woke up in a panic as I looked around me to see where I was and what was happening.

"You're sitting in your own chair in your own house. Now—settle down and get yourself to bed," I mumbled.

Chapter 7

When the alarm blasted its annoying buzz, I wasn't ready to get up. That dream must have really bothered my psyche. Every time I would drift off to sleep, the dream would return, but I never did see what was causing the odor. It certainly smelled like death.

I crawled from beneath my covers so I could face the day head on, even if I needed more restful sleep.

"A shower should get me started," I mumbled as I plodded across the room to the bathroom.

A few minutes later I was knocking on the doors of three different bedrooms to awaken Ryan, Ellen, and Emily so they could get ready for school. Ellen was the first one to enter the kitchen where I had placed boxes of cereal on the counter so they could pick and choose what they each wanted to eat.

"It will be cold cereal today, Ellen. I'm running on a slow bell. I didn't sleep well last night," I said in explanation.

"No problem," Ellen said in response. "Why didn't you sleep?"

"I kept having a dream, maybe I should call it a nightmare. Nightmares are something I'm not used to. I haven't had those since I was a kid, and usually it was after I watched a scary movie. Well, I guess that dream/nightmare was a scary movie," I said with a forced laugh. "Forget about my bad dream. Are you feeling better this morning?" I asked as I remembered the tears she shed the previous evening.

"I'm okay. I do want to go to the dance but I will need to think of a costume to wear," she said as she sounded like her bubbly self again.

"We'll work on that after I get home from work, if you want my help," I said as I gave her a hug.

"Sure, Mom, I really could use your help."

"Did you hear Emily moving around?" I asked Ellen.

"Come to think of it, no, I didn't."

I set my much-needed coffee cup on the counter and walked down the hall to check on Ryan and Emily.

Ryan was always by sleepyhead.

"Come on, Ryan. Up and at'em!" I shouted as I tapped on his door. I kept tapping until I heard a response.

I moved on to Emily's bedroom door but as I started to tap on it, it swung open.

"Em?" I whispered into the dark room.

I reached to the side of the doorway and flicked the switch to illuminate the room. Her bed was made up so I glanced toward her bathroom. It was empty.

Emily was gone!!!

Chapter 8

E llen, come here," I yelled down the hallway toward the kitchen area.

"Just a sec," she responded.

She wasn't moving fast enough for me, so I started walking toward the kitchen.

"Ryan, out here, now!" I shouted as I walked passed his bedroom door.

"Okay! Okay!" he shouted back at me.

When I arrived at the kitchen I started on Ellen.

"Where is your sister?"

"I don't know," she whimpered in response.

"Ryan, do you know where Emily went?" I demanded of my son when he entered the kitchen.

"No, I didn't know she was gone," he sputtered in reply.

"Ellen, why don't you know where she is? You are her twin sister. Please tell me," I pleaded.

"The last time I talked with her she said she was going to meet Tim Riley," Ellen said as she tried not to cry.

"Where and when was she going to meet him?" I demanded as I fought to control my growing temper.

"She didn't say, Mom. Honestly, she didn't tell me. I didn't

19

think she meant it for last night."

"How did she get out without me knowing about it?" I asked.

"I guess she climbed out the window in her bedroom," said Ellen.

"Am I going to have to put bars on the bedroom windows?" I asked Ryan and Ellen. Neither one of them answered me because they knew I didn't mean what I was saying.

"All right. You two eat your breakfasts and get on the school bus. I will look for Emily," I said sadly.

I called Annie, the receptionist at the law office where I worked, to let her know I would be late if I got there at all.

After Ryan and Ellen climbed onto the school bus, I went searching for Emily. I drove to the end of the street to the last house before the house in the woods and knocked on the door.

The door was opened by a tall, thin woman who was a few years older than me.

"Is there a Tim Riley living here?" I asked politely.

"Why do you want to know?" the tall, thin woman responded with a question.

"Is he here?" I asked sharply.

"Who are you?" demanded the tall, thin woman.

"Let's start over. My name is Lindsay Harris. I live down the street from this house. My daughter, Emily, is missing. She was supposed to meet Tim Riley somewhere. I don't know where or when they were to meet. Now—is Tim Riley living here?" I said in a very controlled tone.

"Lindsay, he does live here but he is supposed to be in school right now. I didn't see him leave and he is not here, so I'm guessing he went to school. I work nights so I get home after he goes to school. I checked his room when I got home and he wasn't here," she explained.

"So, you really don't know when he left or if he was even at home last night," I said accusingly.

20

"No, I don't, but he is sixteen years old and doesn't need a baby-sitter," she snapped.

"Again, ma'am, I'm sorry for sounding so short, but my daughter is missing and she may be with him," I said with sincerity,

"Obviously, your daughter needs a baby-sitter," she said sarcastically.

"I was home when she sneaked out a window. Normally, she doesn't do this kind of thing," I said in answer to her sarcasm.

My temper was rising. I knew I had to end the conversation really, really fast before I did something stupid like reach out and slap her silly until he told me what I wanted to hear.

"I will leave you my phone number so you can call me when and if Tim Riley returns home," I said as I handed her a slip of paper with my name and phone number written in bold letters.

"By the way, what is your name?" I asked.

"Nancy."

That was all she was going to tell me so I walked away, dejected, disappointed, and desperate.

Chapter 9

I climbed into my car and just sat there thinking about what I should do next.

My eyes were drawn to the small forest of trees that were positioned in front of me.

"No, she wouldn't have gone there without me," I mumbled, but I was beginning to not believe my own words.

The noise from my cell phone brought me out of my rambling thoughts.

"Hello? Emily?" I said.

"No, this is Jed. Why did you think I was Emily?" he asked with a lilt in his voice.

"She is missing," I blurted in response.

"Since when?"

"Since last night. When I went to get her up for school this morning, she was gone," I explained as I tried to control my angry tears. I didn't know where to direct the anger.

Was I angry with Emily? Was I angry with Tim Riley or the lady who called herself Nancy?

I wasn't sure who deserved the brunt of my anger. All I knew was that I was, again, shedding tears and Jed was the one who was on the other end of the conversation hearing all the sobs.

22

"What happened, Linds?" Jed asked.

"I really don't know," I said between sobs.

"You have to know something," he pressed.

I was finally gaining control of the sobs when I said, "The last time I saw her was when she went to bed last night. I really don't know what happened. Ellen said Emily probably sneaked out to go meet her new friend, Tim Riley. But that was only a guess."

"Where is this Tim Riley? Do you know anything about him?" Jed asked.

"I don't know where he is, but I think Em is with him. He is new to the area, I think, so I don't know anything about him."

"You think? What's that about?" Jed asked.

"Ellen said he used to live in the house in the woods years ago but that was what she was told by some of her classmates who could have been making it up."

"Did you check his home?" he asked.

"Yes, but he wasn't there and the lady, Nancy, who answered the door wasn't very forthcoming with information," I said sadly.

"Do you want me to come keep you company while you try to find her?"

"You don't have to do that, Jed."

"I know, but I want to help."

"Okay. Great. Come on. You can go with me to check on the house in the woods. I really don't want to go there alone."

"I'll be about an hour getting there."

"See you when you get here."

The house in the woods was still trying to lure me into its clutches even though it was hidden from view behind the trees.

I started my car and moved the gear to drive. I had to go toward the trees so I could turn around and head back toward my house. When I pulled into the spot to turn around, I turned off the engine, and crawled out of my car.

"Why am I doing this?" I mumbled. "I need to wait for Jed."

I walked through the expanse of trees and aimed my body to-

23

ward the front porch. I moved slowly, looking around, so I could take into my memory everything around me.

When I climbed the first of four steps leading to the front porch, I paused to listen.

I heard nothing, absolutely nothing.

There should be birds flying around in the trees making a racket, but it was totally silent. I saw no birds, no squirrels, no chipmunks, no rabbits, and, thankfully, no rats. I decided to turn around to leave. I was afraid to continue; the silence worried me too much.

I ran back to my car and headed for home to make some telephone calls.

Chapter 10

"Could you tell me if Tim Riley and Emily Harris are in school today?" I asked the not too interested young lady who answered the telephone at the high school.

"I'm sorry but I can't give out that information," she responded.

"This is Lindsay Harris and I'm Emily's mother," I said but was interrupted before I could continue.

"Oh, Mrs. Harris. Emily didn't come to school today. Didn't you know?" she asked.

"I was afraid of that. How about Tim Riley?" I asked again.

"I'm not supposed to tell you that he isn't here either. Is there a problem?" whispered the young lady who was totally interested in the conversation at this time.

"Who am I speaking with?" I asked the young lady.

"This is Martha, Mrs. H. I'm a friend of both of your girls."

"Yes, I remember you. You've been to my house a couple of times. Do you know Tim Riley?" I asked.

"Not much, he is new to the school. He's been here about two weeks, I think," she whispered conspiratorially.

"Martha, write down my phone number and call me if you hear from or see Emily," I said in a motherly tone.

25

"Yes, ma'am, I sure will."

As soon as I hung up the receiver, Jed was knocking at my front door.

"Have you found her yet?" he asked when I pulled the door open to let him inside.

"No, I'm really getting worried. No one knows where she is," I said with a sigh. I had given up crying because I was no longer angry; at this point, I was scared.

"You've checked with the school, haven't you?" he asked.

"Of course, but no luck. Neither of them were there today."

"So you think she is with this Tim Riley boy?"

"Yes, I do, but I don't know where they would have gone."

"Where is the house in the woods that you want to check out?" Jed asked.

"At the end of my street, but it is sort of a scary place. I've been to the front porch twice alone and was scared away both times. If you go with me, we can go inside and check it out."

"You've been twice? What scared you the first time?" Jed asked.

"A flash of light blinded me so much that I couldn't go inside. All I did was push open the front door. The second time was total and complete silence that worried me," I explained.

"Both of those actions sound a bit strange; let's go see what happens this time," Jed said with evident excitement.

The telephone jarred me so much that I jerked to attention before I answered it.

"Hey, Marnie," I said after I looked at the caller ID.

"What's going on, Linds? Why didn't you go to work today? Are you not feeling well?" Marnie asked without allowing me to answer the first question.

"Emily's missing," I said in explanation.

"Do you want me to come home from work to help you find her?" Marnie asked.

26

"Jed's here but I can use all the help I can get. Did you find out anything about the house in the woods?"

"Yes, bunches. I'll tell you about it when I get there."

"You won't get into trouble for leaving work early, will you?" I asked.

"No, I'll tell them it's a family emergency. You are my honorary sister, aren't you?"

"Sure," I said as she disconnected the line.

Now, the only one of my close friends missing was Annie, the receptionist from work. *I'll call her later*, I thought.

I made a pot of coffee so we could discuss a strategy.

I wanted Jed to go with me to the house in the woods. I was hoping Marnie wouldn't mind staying at the house waiting for Ryan and Ellen to get home. Maybe she could get some more information out of Ellen. Ellen might be a little more open with a woman who wasn't her mother.

When Marnie arrived, I left her sitting in the living room while Jed and I took off down the street to visit the house in the woods.

"I'll tell you everything I found out when you get back," Marnie said as we closed the door.

27

Chapter 11

G et in my car, Linds. You just need to tell me where to go," he said with a grin.

"Just keep driving straight the way you are headed and you will run right into the woods. The house is a few hundred feet beyond that cluster of trees in a large clearing that is well hidden from the road."

"Sure is isolated, isn't it?" he commented.

"You could say that. Just keep going and see how isolated it is."

"There are the trees. Now—where do I park?" Jed asked.

"In front of the trees in that graveled space. Then we have to walk."

"Is it far?" he asked.

"No, let's go. It won't take long to get there," I said as I led the way.

The house loomed up in front of us like a giant spectacle. It was dark, uninviting, and emanating an aura of doom and gloom.

"Wow," said Jed as he stared at the house.

"See what I mean about scary," I said as I, too, stared at the huge mansion-like house.

We both had come to a complete stop. I motioned for him to

28

listen to his surroundings.

The birds were singing and flying from tree to tree. Squirrels were skittering to the trunks, up and down, and all around them.

"This was not happening earlier today," I said. "You can hear the noises of nature now, but there was complete and total silence a couple of hours ago."

"What would have caused that?" asked Jed.

"I don't know. Maybe there was someone or something hanging around here that the animals and birds were afraid of," I answered.

"What would that be?" Jed asked.

"Maybe something not natural," I said, trying not to say what I really thought.

"What would not natural be? A ghost? A demon? An evil spirit?" said Jed in exasperation.

"Any or all of them," I answered.

"Get serious, Linds."

"I am serious, and I tell you I am scared to be here," I said softly.

"Don't be afraid. I'm right here with you," he said with a snicker.

"My hero," I sighed with all the sarcasm I could emit.

We started walking again and when we climbed up the first step of the porch, the atmosphere seemed to change.

The silence was back.

"Listen," I whispered to Jed.

"What happened to all of the nature sounds?" asked an astonished Jed.

"Weird, isn't it?" I said as I looked into his eyes. I wanted to see if any of this strange stuff was affecting him.

We moved on up the steps and reached the front door.

"The flash happened when I pushed open the front door," I whispered. "the door was slightly ajar like it is now."

Jed reached his hand forward to give the door a shove.

"Bang? You are dead!" said a voice from inside the house.

A flash of light radiated from the interior and we were both blinded by the sudden bright light.

I reached out to grab hold of Jed's arm for comfort and reassurance.

"You were right, Linds. There was a flash of light," he said. "Have your eyes cleared up yet? Where did that voice come from? Did you hear that statement about being dead before when you pushed open the door?"

"No, there was no voice the first time, just the flash. My eyes haven't cleared up yet. How about yours? Can you see anything?" I asked.

"Just dots, lot of dots."

I hung onto to his arm. I was afraid to let go for fear that he would disappear. My mind kept telling me that he was the only little bit of reality around me.

I blinked my eyes again and again until finally the swirling dots subsided. That's when I focused in on the overwhelming darkness. It looked like the interior of the whole house had been painted black.

"Jed, I'm no longer seeing swirling dots. All I see now is black," I said in a whisper.

"Same here," he said softly. "Maybe we should leave while we can. We need a flashlight before we can do any more investigating. I really want to know where that voice and that flash came from, don't you?"

"Great idea, let's get out of here and come back later," I said.

The door was open slightly so was walked toward the only light that could be seen, and that was outside.

Chapter 12

Jed and I were silent during the short ride to my house. The kids were already home from school, so I didn't want to say anything about what had happened at the house in the woods except for the fact that Emily was not there from what we could see.

"Marnie, I'm going to get supper ready, consisting of soup, sandwiches, and chips; then you can tell us all about the history of the house before I start searching for Emily again. I guess I should call the police and get them involved."

Ryan and Ellen were very pleased with my menu choices because they knew they could eat in front of the televisions in each of their rooms.

I was ravenous and a piled high sandwich was going to make me happy. I guess the adrenaline rush of being frightened a couple of times earlier in the day had activated my hunger drive. Jed and Marnie helped themselves so they, too, could get passed the necessity of filling their bodies with fuel.

"Linds, are you ready for me to begin my tale of the house in the woods?" Marnie asked.

"Yes, please begin," I said with interest.

"That house is really, really old. It was built over a hundred years ago. Does it look that old, Jed?" Marnie asked.

31

"No, not really. It must have been well maintained over the years," he replied.

"Well, I don't know how because it has been empty for many years. According to the records I found in the courthouse, it was built before the depression of the 1920's hit, which was a good thing; otherwise, the construction may not have been completed."

"How long has it been empty?" I asked. "I know that Ellen told me that Tim Riley had lived in the house. Tim is sixteen, so it has to be less than sixteen years earlier."

"The records seem to indicate it has been empty since the construction was completed. The story is that the lady of the house caught her husband with another woman and shot them both in the house. I haven't had a chance to go back through the old trial records to find out if that was true or not. Supposedly the members of the families of the husband or wife wanted nothing to do with the house because it was haunted. You didn't see any ghosts, did you?" Marnie asked with a smile turning up the corners of her mouth.

"Are you sure no one has lived there?" I asked.

"If they have, there is no record of it at the courthouse. Of course, there may not be any record if the property hasn't been sold or transferred to anyone other than the original owners, who are long dead. I really don't know why the county hasn't sold it for back unpaid taxes."

"The young man that Emily is supposed to be with was said to have lived in that house when he was a little boy," I said in explanation.

"The only people who could tell you that for sure are the utility companies. I'm sure they would have had power bills to pay for their electricity usage," said Marnie.

"How am I going to find that out?" I asked Marnie.

"You work for a lawyer. Tell them you need the information for a title search. Maybe some poor soul, like me, will take pity on you and give you a name or two," Marnie said with a grin.

I decided it was time for me to call all of Emily's friends with help from Ellen.

Ellen called everyone she could think of but had no luck at all with finding the whereabouts of Emily or Tim.

The only thing left for me to do was call the police.

Chapter 13

I need to report a missing child," I told the officer who answered the phone at the Stillwell Police Department.

"How long has she been missing?" he asked

"She disappeared sometime last night," I answered.

"How old is she" he asked.

"14," I said. I knew I was going to get the run around because of the fact she was a teenager.

"Did she run away from home, ma'am?" he asked with a cynical tone.

"No sir, she did not run away. She had no reason to run away. She is missing and I believe there is a young man named Tim Riley with her. He is also missing."

"Did they run away together?" he asked using that same cynical tone.

"No, they were investigating the haunted house on my street and they just disappeared."

"You need to come to the station to file a report," he said coolly.

"Can't you send an officer to my house and I will tell him where I think they vanished from?"

"Yes ma'am, I will send an officer as soon as one becomes available," he said smugly.

34

"You do that," I snapped.

I hung up the receiver with a controlled hand, but I so wanted to slam it down to vent my frustration.

"What did they say?" asked Marnie.

"They are calling her a runaway. That means they aren't going to do much of anything," I said angrily.

"Why don't you call your boss? I'm sure Wayne could get them moving. He is a well-known and respected lawyer in this town," suggested Marnie.

"I really don't want him meddling in my business. I work for him and I'd rather not owe him, if you know what I mean," I explained.

"Okay, but he can get them moving," said Marnie.

"Jed could probably do the same thing, you know," I said.

"How?" asked Jed.

"Tell them you are a newspaper reporter checking on the missing teenagers. I'm sure they wouldn't want any kind of bad press," I said as I glanced at Jed.

"Yeah, that might work. I'll give them a call from my cell phone so they won't think you put me up to this," Jed said.

Marnie and I sat on the sofa while Jed paced the room as he talked with the officer who answered the telephone at the Stillwell Police Department.

"I'm checking on what progress has been made on the two missing teenagers. I'm Jed Thompson from the Bristol Newspaper and we are doing a feature story on the missing kids."

He was doing a wonderful job of embellishing. Of course, he would, because he was a writer.

The conversation exchange was short.

"Well, what did he say?" I asked.

"No comment, but they are investigating and they will give me a call when they uncover any details," he said with a smile. "They will probably have an officer at your door soon."

35

Chapter 14

A knock at the door caused me to spin around and look at Jed. "That can't be the police, can it?" I whispered.

"It might be but I just hung up the phone. That sure would be fast if it is," he said skeptically.

I pulled the door open and stood face to face with a teenager, definitely not a police person.

"Hi, who are you?" I asked.

"My name is Mike. Tim Riley asked me to give you a message," he said softly.

"Come in and tell us all," I said as I motioned for him to enter the living room.

He hesitated. He really looked like a scared puppy. He lowered his eyes to the floor and walked through the entrance.

"Okay, Mike, what did Tim Riley want you to tell me?" I said as I urged him to speak.

"He said to tell you he and Emily are okay and not to look for them. They will come home as soon as they can but it might take a while."

"Why?" I demanded.

"What do you mean?" he stammered.

"Why will it take a while?" I asked.

36

"He didn't say."

"What else did he say?" I demanded.

"Nothing except to make sure the cops didn't get involved," blustered Mike.

"Are they in danger?" I asked.

"I don't know."

"How and when did he tell you to give me the message?" I asked in a softer voice. I could see Mike was getting nervous and antsy.

"He called me after school today," he answered.

"Did he use a cell phone?" I probed.

"I guess. I don't know for sure."

"Do you have a cell phone?" I asked.

"No, he called me at home."

"Does your home phone record the numbers for those who called?" I asked.

"No, we don't have caller ID."

"What is your last name, Mike?"

"Simpson, I live over on the next street," he answered.

"Where?" Jed asked.

"2597 Hurricane Avenue."

"The police will be visiting you," said Jed, "I'm sure they will have some questions for you."

"But he said not to call the cops," sputtered a red faced Mike.

"Too late, we've already done that," I said sternly.

"I'll have to tell him," he said indignantly.

"How are you going to tell him?" I demanded.

"He'll call me again. He wants to know what you have to say," he said with determination.

"When will he do that?" asked Marnie.

"In about an hour but I have to go home to answer the call," he said smugly.

"You can go home but I'm going with you," said Marnie.

"You can't do that," he stammered.

"I can and I will," Marnie snapped.

Mike abruptly turned and ran out of the door that I had not closed when he entered.

Marnie sprang up from her sitting position on the sofa and sprinted after him. I watched them run and realized he was not going to lose Marnie. She was right on his heels.

Flashing blue lights caught my attention as a police car turned onto my street. I walked to the edge of my front yard to get the officer's attention.

When the officer climbed out of the car, I was surprised to see a female. I knew there were supposed to be female officers in the town department, but they were few and far between.

"Hello, Mrs. Harris, I'm Officer Whitt," she said as she extended her hand.

"It's Ms. Harris. The mister is long gone. Please call me Lindsay," I said politely. "Tell me about your daughter and her friend," said Officer Whitt.

"Come on in and you can have a seat. Then we can talk," I said as I ushered her into my house.

I introduced her to Jed.

"You're the newspaper report asking about the missing teens," Officer Whitt stated.

"Yes ma'am. Lindsay and her kids are friends of mine. She is my source for feature stories in this area," he explained.

"Well, your little telephone call worked. It got me here. I need to get some more information about you daughter," she said as she looked at me.

"She's fourteen and she looks like Ellen who is sitting right there," I said as I pointed to a side chair. "They are identical twins."

"We will need a recent photograph and the general details of height, weight, hair color, eye color, and anything else that identifies her specifically."

I grabbed the photograph of both girls with Ryan positioned

38

between them and removed it from the frame. It had been taken the previous month so it was the newest one I had.

"Does she look like this now? She hasn't changed her hair to blue or anything strange," asked Officer Whitt.

"She looks like the photo and no, she does not have blue hair," I said with a smile. I knew that was the trend. I had seen girls walking around with blue, green, purple, and pink hair. That was something I hoped my girls would not want to do.

"Where is it you think that your daughter and her friend, Tim Riley, would have gone?" asked Officer Whitt.

"When I called earlier, I told the person who answered the phone that I believed they went to investigate the empty house at the end of this street and they never came home."

"The house at the end of this street is occupied," said Officer Whitt.

"No ma'am, it is not. I'm talking about the house in the woods," I explained.

"I didn't know there was a house in the woods."

"Most people don't know it's there," I said.

"I will check it out and get back with you if I find anything," said Officer Whitt as she stood to leave.

I watched Officer Whitt pull her vehicle from my driveway and head toward the house in the woods. I wanted so very much to be with her as she investigated the place that had already scared me twice.

Chapter 15

After the police officer cleared out, I sat on the sofa next to Jed and cried.

I wasn't a very emotional woman ordinarily, but the thought that one of my children was in danger scared me to the point of tears. I could feel the tide of danger rising and I didn't know how to stop it; and to be truthful, I didn't know what the danger was.

"Jed, we called everyone including the police. I just can't continue to sit here and do nothing. Tell me what I should do," I pleaded.

"Let's go find Marnie and Mike. Ellen can lock the doors and stay here in case Emily comes home. They can call us if she shows up," Jed said as he tried to pull me from my tears.

"Yes, let's do that. That kid is not telling us everything. Maybe Tim has called by now," I said with a forced smile.

Jed drove slowly down my street. We both swiveled our heads side to side searching for a sign of the missing teens.

"What was that address again?" I said as I searched for house numbers after Jed turned onto Hurricane Street.

"Do you see it yet?" he asked.

"No—wait a minute. There it is," I said as I pointed to a small house that had been painted bright blue.

"Why would anyone want to paint a perfectly fine house bright blue?" asked Jed with a grimace.

"Maybe that was the only color they had," I said sincerely.

"There aren't any lights on in the house and it's almost dark," said Jed as he turned the car onto the driveway.

"I don't see anyone moving around inside or out," I said in response. "Marnie should be here. I didn't see her walking along the road."

"Let's go knock on the door to be sure," said Jed as he exited the car.

We walked up the sidewalk that was in disrepair with cracks and chips covering most of the path.

Even though the exterior of the house had been painted bright blue, the floor of the front porch appeared to be unsafe. I was afraid to walk on the damaged planks that made up the walking area. There were some gaping holes through which I could see the dried ground below.

"Be careful where you step," I whispered to Jed.

We moved forward to the door and Jed knocked loudly. We waited, but there was no answer to the knock.

I moved over carefully to my right so I could peek into a window. I held my hands up to the sides of my face to help me focus on what was in front of me without any interference from my surroundings.

"I can't see anything," I said to Jed.

"No people?" Jed asked.

"Nothing, no people, no furniture, nothing," I said.

"What?" Jed said as he moved over next to me. "This is the correct address, isn't it?"

"It's the one he gave us but I guess he lied," I said in response.

"Now, we've got another missing person from our lives. Where did Marnie get off to?"

"She's got to be around here somewhere," I answered and I glanced to see if any of the neighbors were home.

"There are some lights on in the house across the street. Let's go see if they have seen Marnie," I suggested.

We hurried across the street leaving the car where it was parked in the driveway of the empty house. Jed knocked and the door was quickly answered by a tall, dark haired man in his middle forties, I guessed. He was pretty close to me in age, judging from his appearance.

"I'm Lindsay Harris and this is Jed Thompson. We are looking for a friend that came running through here. Her name is Marnie and she was running after a young man names Mike Simpson. Have you seen either one of them run by here?" I asked.

"Why was she chasing Mike?" he demanded.

"That's a long story and it's about two missing teenagers and now, Mike and Marnie can't be located," Jed explained.

"I did see Mike and he was being chased by some wild woman. Why was she chasing him?" he asked again.

"Mike was supposed to get a phone call from a young man who might know where my daughter is. Please tell us if you know anything about either of them," I pleaded.

"Like I said, I saw them running by here. I don't know where they were going. I don't believe either of them live on this street," he said smugly.

"Do you know where Mike Simpson lives?" I asked.

"Like I said, he doesn't live on this street but I have seen him in the neighborhood," he answered in a huff. He seemed to be tired of answering my questions.

"Thank you sir. We won't bother you anymore," Jed said as he tried to steer me away from the man.

I wanted to just jump on top of him and beat the information I knew he had right out of him.

Chapter 16

Go get in the car, Linds," said Jed gruffly.

"No, I want to pound on that smug son of a gun," I shouted.

"Stop it. Getting mad isn't going to help," he said as he kept pushing me toward the car parked across the street.

"He knows something. I can feel it in my bones," I whined,

"We'll keep an eye on him. I just don't want him to know we are watching him," said Jed.

"How are we going to do that? He will see us," I asked.

"Look, that's your house right there," he said as he pointed beyond the man's house. "We can watch him from your back yard, can't we?"

"Why didn't I think of that?" I asked as I scanned my own house from a distance.

"Too much on your mind. Now, what do you want to do next?" Jed asked.

"Just drive up and down the street in this neighborhood. I need to be doing something. I need to be looking for them, all of them," I said with a sigh.

My cell phone jangled. After a quick glance, I knew it was Marnie calling.

"Where are you?" I asked without even saying hello.

"Well, hello to you, too," said a snide Marnie.

"Marnie, where are you? Jed and I have been driving up and down the streets trying to find you," I said with concern apparent in my voice.

"I was following that snot nosed kid. He sure did lead me on a merry chase. He finally stopped at a house on your street and I went in right behind him," Marnie explained.

"Did you find out anything?" I asked.

"Yes, and it was nothing that will help us find the missing kids," Marnie said.

"What did you find out?" I asked.

"That kid is useless. The so-called phone call came but it wasn't from Tim Riley. It was from a girl and not Emily. They were trying to get money from you, Lindsay. They don't know where Tim and Emily are."

"If I could get my hands on that Mike Simpson, I would strangle him," I said angrily.

"Just forget about them and we will focus on Emily," said Jed as he was, again, trying to calm me down. My temper was truly too short.

"Where are you now, Marnie?" I asked again.

"At your house," she replied.

I glanced side to side searching the street as Jed drove back to my house. I was getting so worried, and I didn't know what my next step should be.

"Don't worry, Linds. We will find her and she will be just fine," said Jed when he saw my wrinkled brow.

"I just want to know why she sneaked out of the house to meet that guy. I'm sure it's not a boy/girl thing. Emily has never expressed much interest in boys like Ellen has."

"I noticed she was different from her twin, but that is a good thing, isn't it?" asked Jed.

"Yes, I guess so, but they look so much alike, you would think

44

that they would act alike, but that couldn't be further from the truth."

"We're here. Let's see what Marnie has to say," Jed said as he pulled into the driveway.

Marnie was sitting on the sofa with Ellen and Ryan attentively listening to everything she had to say. They looked so totally engrossed that I hesitated about interrupting their little talk session.

"Hey, Linds," said Marnie as her attention was turned away from the kids.

"I know you haven't been back to work to do some investigating, but I'm hoping you have some more news for me," I said in a pleading tone.

"Well, as a matter of fact, I do," Marnie said with a smile.

"Okay, give. What else?"

"You need to talk with your children. They have some things they need to tell you," Marnie said as she stared directly at Ryan and then Ellen.

"Okay, guys, what secrets have you been keeping?" I asked in a motherly tone. If I was too harsh, I was afraid they would just clam up and keep the secrets forever. "Who wants to go first?"

Both of my children looked at each other. Neither of them spoke for a few seconds.

"You go ahead, Ryan. I think you need to start it out," whispered Ellen.

Ryan swallowed hard and again was silent as he stared at the floor.

"What is it, Ryan?" I urged.

He looked up at me and I could see fear dancing in his eyes.

"What are you afraid of, Ryan?"

"I—I—I, nothing. I ain't afraid of nothing," he stammered.

"Yes you are. I can see the fear in your eyes. Tell me what it is so I can help," I pleaded softly.

"It's about that house in the woods," he said solemnly.

"What about the house in the woods?"

"It's haunted and I think the ghost has Emily," he said as he sought back tears.

"Why do you think it's haunted?" I probed.

"Me and a couple of friends went exploring one Saturday afternoon when I went to Billy's house with your permission. Billy's mom wasn't home so we went for a walk. She said that would be okay, according to Billy, and we decided to stop in at the house in the woods," he said. He paused and took a deep breath.

"Go on," I said.

"We had heard some of the scary stories that had been going around the school, so we wanted to see for ourselves," he said as he stared at his feet.

"Look at me, Ryan, and tell me what happened," I said in a sterner tone.

He moved his head up to look at me straight on and said, "We saw a ghost, mom. We saw a real ghost and he chased us away."

"What did this ghost look like?" I asked.

"He was really big. He was dressed in white and he had splashes of red on the white that looked like blood. He raised his arms in the air and his fingers looked all bloody. He chased us until we got to the edge of the clearing. That was the last time I saw him but I kept running and I didn't want to look back. I was afraid he would catch us and kill us," said Ryan excitedly.

"Did he look like a real man all dressed up in white clothes?" I asked.

"No, no, he looked like a ghost. That's what I saw, a real ghost."

"Okay, Ryan. I believe you. Now, Ellen it's your turn," I said as I looked at Ellen.

"Carolyn Potter and I were doing the same thing that Ryan was doing. We were trying to figure out if the rumors were true," Ellen said softly.

"What did you find out?" I asked pointedly.

"We were already scared to begin with when we got there. It doesn't take much of the supernatural stuff to get me scared, so you had to know I was scared," Ellen said.

"Okay, okay, you were scared. Please go on," I said as I urged her to tell her story a little bit faster.

"It was almost dark, and it was so cloudy that there weren't any stars. The moon was just a little slip of a thing that kept darting in and out of the racing clouds. We brought flashlights with us just in case we needed them. That was a good thing," Ellen said as she paused to get her words straight in her mind. I could see her eyes darting back and forth as if she were reading what she was telling me from a piece of paper.

"Go on," I said.

"We stepped up on the porch and waited for something to reach out and grab us. When it didn't, we moved to the front door. The house was empty, or so we thought; therefore, we didn't knock. Instead, we turned the knob and took a step inside."

"Did you see and flashes of light?" I asked as I interrupted her train of thought.

"No, it was totally black so I flicked the switch on my flashlight. I shined it around quickly but I wasn't seeing anything or anyone that I could recognize and then the beam of light disappeared. It went out. There was no reason for the darkness. I flicked the switch back and forth but no more light appeared. Carolyn's flashlight did the same thing. We both took it as a sign that we should leave. So, that's what we did."

"Did you get chased?" I asked.

"No, but we didn't hang around to see if anyone was after us. We just ran as fast as we could," she said excitedly.

"You didn't see a flash of light from inside the house when you entered?" I asked.

"No."

I sat and thought for a moment before I asked, "Do you think Emily is in the house?"

Ellen answered, "Yes, ma'am. I think she and Tim are both in that house."

"Ryan?"

"I think that ghost has both of them," he answered.

Chapter 17

"Marnie, did you learn anything more about Mike Simpson, the boy you were chasing?" I asked. I was trying so hard to make the pieces fit but that wasn't happening.

"No, just what I've already told you. He was just out to make some money at your expense," Marnie answered.

"Ryan, have you ever met Mike Simpson? I'm sure he is a few years older than you, but you might know him from somewhere."

"No, ma'am. He probably hangs out with some of Ellen's and Emily's friends."

"Ellen, do you know Mike Simpson?" I asked. She was scooting down in her seat trying to avoid my prying eyes. "Out with it, Ellen."

"Mike Simpson is in my math class. He seems like a really nice boy. At least, I like him, but he has a steady girlfriend and would barely talk with me. I've never seen him talk with Emily but I'm sure he knows we are sisters. The whole school knows we are identical twins," she said with a hint of disgust.

"What about his family? Have you ever met his mom and Dad? What were they like?" I asked.

"I've seen his mom once or twice and she is really a piece of work. She has tattoos everywhere and piercings in places you wouldn't believe."

"What about his father?" I probed.

"Rumor has it that he is in prison," Ellen answered.

"Do you know why?"

"He is some kind of a con artist. He cheated some old people out of every cent they had," Ellen explained.

"The apple doesn't fall far from the tree," I said.

"What does that mean?" asked Ryan.

"Mike Simpson learned from his father how to cheat people out of their money. That is what he was trying to do to us," I explained.

"Ellen, Tim Riley is in some of your classes, right?" I asked.

"Yes."

"What do you know about him?" I asked.

"Nothing, really. He is new in the school so he hasn't had very much time to make anyone mad at him. That's usually where the talk, good or bad, gets started," she said.

"Emily said he used to live in that house. Did you know that?" I asked Ellen.

"Not until she said so. He is a little strange, you know," she whispered.

"What do you mean by s 'little strange'?" I asked.

"He dresses all in black. You know, like those gothic people," she said.

"Anything else?"

"He has long, brown hair that he dyes black, and his skin is pale like he has been really sick," she explained.

"Why would Emily be interested in anyone like that?" I asked.

"Because of the house, I think," Ellen said. "She was really interested in the house in the woods. You know she has been there before, don't you?"

"I guessed as much. Why all of the interest?" I asked.

"She likes that sort of thing. It doesn't seem to scare her as much as it does me. We are so different in that way."

"Were you with her when she visited the house?" I asked sternly.

"No, ma'am. She always went with someone else or maybe even alone. I would never go there alone," Ellen said with a shutter.

"I know what you mean," I said as I remembered my visit when I was alone.

"Ellen, Ryan, it's getting late. You need to go to bed," I said to my wide-awake children.

"It's Friday, Mom. We don't have to go to school tomorrow. Can't we stay up a while longer?" asked Ryan.

"Yes, but stay up in your rooms. I want to do some adult talking with Jed and Marnie," I explained.

Chapter 18

Lindsay, I've been sitting here listening to you cross examine your children, and I think you are pretty darn good at getting to the truth. I'm like the kids, I think Emily is mixed up with that house in some strange way. I think we need to do some more checking into that house in the woods," said Jed.

"The police said they would check it out. I think I should call them and see what they have to say. They may have found out something new about the missing kids," I said.

"Good idea."

"I wonder if I should call them now?"

"Why not? Cops work twenty-four hours a day," said Jed with a smile.

When I entered the police department telephone number, not 9-1-1, it took them a few rings to answer the call.

"Hi, this is Lindsay Harris. May I speak with Officer Whitt?" I asked.

"One moment, I need to check to see if she is still here," said the gentleman who answered the telephone.

I was positioned on my end of the silent telephone line as I waited for Officer Whitt to get answer my call.

"Hello, this is Officer Whitt," said a strong sounding female

52

voice.

"Officer Whitt, this is Lindsay Harris, the mother of the missing girl, Emily Harris. You said you were going to check out the house in the woods to see if there was any indication that Emily and Tim Riley were there or even if they had been there. Did you get a chance to do that?" I asked hesitantly.

There was a long pause that forced me to speak again.

"Officer Whitt? Are you still on the line?" I asked.

"Yes, yes, Mrs. Harris, I'm here," she answered softly.

"Is there a problem, Officer Whitt?" I asked also in a hushed tone. "Please call me Lindsay."

"Okay, Lindsay, I will tell you what I experienced at that house in the woods but I really don't want my fellow officers to hear this. Wait for a moment while I go to an unoccupied office where I can have a bit of privacy. I am putting you on hold for a few moments," Officer Whitt said as there was a click followed by silence.

When it was apparent that I was on hold, Jed asked, "What's going on?"

"I'm on hold because she wants to talk to me without eavesdroppers," I whispered as I held my hand over the speaker.

Another click could be heard followed by, "Lindsay?"

"Yes, yes, I'm here."

"How much do you know about that house in the woods and what goes on there?" Officer Whitt asked.

"I just found out about the house a day ago. I only know, rumor wise, what the kids have told me. I have been to the house twice and was scared away both times," I explained.

"Tell me about the two visits," Officer Whitt said softly.

I mentioned the flash of light that occurred both times, with the addition of 'bang you're dead' and the total darkness.

"Sounds a bit like what I encountered," said the officer.

"Really?"

"Yes, when I approached the place after exiting my vehicle, I didn't expect anything to happen in an empty, deserted house. I had my gun out and ready just in case I ran into a vagrant with a grudge; but instead, I saw a flash of light followed by complete darkness."

"Did you hear anyone speak?" I asked.

"No, I can't say that I did because I was too busy shouting for whoever was in there to come out with his hands up," she explained.

"Did you leave then?" I asked.

"I sure did. I didn't have my flashlight with me and I knew I couldn't look around inside without it. I just turned and left, ever so grateful that I was able to leave," she said in a barely audible tone.

"I know how you felt," I said. "Have you found any more information about where Emily Harris and Tim Riley could be? Do you think they might be at that house—somewhere hidden in the bowels of the structure?" I asked as I anticipated a negative response.

"I truthfully don't know. I plan to go back to the house tomorrow afternoon. I am going to have a coworker with me. He will be one of the big, bold, muscular males that I work with here. He might get scared off just like me; but, I will feel a bit safer with his company," Officer Whitt said with a sigh.

"What time will you be at the house in the woods?" I asked hesitantly.

"Right after lunch, say about one o'clock. Why do you ask?"

"I want to be there. My two friends and I would like to join you in your investigation," I said. I was so afraid she would object to a civilian tagging along in her search.

"Yes, Lindsay, I think it would be good for you to be there. Just remember, I don't know what we will run in to," the officer said with encouragement.

"I'll see you tomorrow," I responded.

Chapter 19

I guess we are all going to the house in the woods," said Marnie as soon as I ended my phone call.

"That we are," I said with enthusiasm.

"What if she isn't there? What if Emily isn't anywhere near that house? What then?" asked Jed.

"I can't answer that. I don't know what else to do. I feel it in my heart and soul that she is in that house—somewhere," I said as I fought back tears.

"I'm going to go home so I can get some sleep, and I will be back tomorrow morning. Call me if you find out anything before then and I'll come right back. Okay, Lindsay?" asked Jed.

"Yes, yes, no problem. Marnie, you need to go home and get some rest, too," I said.

"Are you sure you will be all right?" asked Marnie.

"Yes, no problem. I have my kids, Ryan and Ellen, here to keep me company. I will call both of you if I hear anything at all. I promise," I said with a forced smile.

Jed and Marnie left and I was sitting in the living room with my mind rambling on to what might be happening to Emily.

"Mom, Mom, come here. There is something you need to see on the computer," shouted Ryan.

"What?" I asked.

"Look at this," said Ryan as he pointed to the computer screen.

"Is that Emily?" I screamed.

"It looks like her," said Ryan.

"Where is this coming from?" I asked nervously.

"I don't know, Mom. I entered Emily's name into the search engine and this is what popped up," explained Ryan.

"How can we find out where this is coming from?" I asked.

"Maybe the police can do that. I don't know how to complete a deep dive into the Internet. They do. They have special programs for that," explained Ryan.

"She's not moving around. That looks like a still photograph to me." I said. "Can you tell where that picture might have been taken?"

"No, not really. Maybe in an old deserted house—like the house in the woods at the end of our street," said Ryan.

"Yes, that's a possibility. Have you been inside that house to see what the individual rooms look like?" I asked Ryan.

"No, but maybe Ellen has," answered Ryan.

I stuck my head out of Ryan's bedroom and shouted for Ellen. She appeared in front of me and I asked her to look the picture on Ryan's computer screen.

"Is that my sister?" she asked excitedly.

"We think so," I answered. "Do you know where that picture might have been snapped?"

"No ma'am. Why would you think I would know that?" she said in a huff.

"I don't know that you do. I'm just asking, that's all," I said as I tried to calm her flaring temper.

"I told you we ran away. We were afraid to go inside because of the flashing light followed by the darkness," Ellen explained.

"I thought maybe you went back another time that you didn't

56

mention," I said softly.

"No, I did not. I have no idea where that picture was taken but I bet it was inside the God-awful house," she said angrily.

"I'm going to go call the police, Ryan. I want you to tell them how you found the picture as soon as I get them on the telephone," I said as I left Ryan's room and headed for the living room where the house phone line was located.

"This is Lindsay Harris, mother of Emily Harris the missing girl. Could I speak to someone who has access to the Internet? There is a photograph of my daughter posted on a website," I explained excitedly.

"One moment please. I will transfer you to Detective Baldwin," said the professional sounding voice that answered my call.

"Detective Baldwin here," said a man who sounded like he was interrupted from whatever he was working on and didn't appreciate the disruption.

"Sir, my name is Lindsay Harris, mother of the missing Emily Harris, and I think there is something on the computer you need to see with regard to the investigation," I explained in a flurry of words. I was tired of repeating the same story over and over again.

"Where do I look?" Detective Baldwin asked.

"I'll put my son, Ryan, on the line so he can tell you how to find the photograph," I said as I handed the telephone receiver to Ryan.

As Ryan instructed the detective on the location of the photograph, I took the time to call Jed's cell phone from my cell phone to let him know what was happening so he, too, could look up the photograph. I thought perhaps with his newspaper background, he might know how to find the location of the website that was blasting her picture on the Internet for the world to see.

My next phone call went to Marnie so could contact her friends and coworkers who might be able to track down the website because of their connections through the commonwealth attorney's office. I had it in my mind that if I had all three investigations going at the same time, maybe one of them could uncover the truth.

"Mom, Mom, it's gone. They took it down. The picture is not there any longer," Ryan shouted excitedly.

I looked at the laptop and there was nothing there except an error message indicating the transmission had been removed.

"Why did they do that?" I asked Ryan not really expecting an explanation.

"Too many people were popping up on the website. He must have been scared off. He was afraid he could be traced," said my smart eleven-year-old son.

"Now what?" I asked.

"We wait. Something else might come up on a different website," said Ryan. "Maybe the police had enough time to track the website. I hope they did but don't hold your breath. They might not have been able to find it. It could have been beamed from many different foreign servers," said Ryan.

"Where did you learn all of this stuff?" I asked Ryan.

"School, friends, books, and television. This information can be found everywhere," he said with the smile of someone who had just revealed a huge secret.

Chapter 20

I remained in the living room close to the telephone, just in case someone called me with information about Emily. But, my real reason for staying close to the phone was that I hoped Emily would call me and tell me she was okay and this whole ordeal was just a joke, a prank, and none of it was true.

That didn't happen.

The phone did not ring and I slept fitfully in the recliner.

By five o-clock I was tired of trying to make myself go back to sleep, so I decided to shower and get ready for the new day. I puttered around in the kitchen, washing dirty dishes and looking for breakfast foods to prepare for Ryan and Ellen. I made a bit extra for Marnie and Jed, just in case they hadn't eaten.

At seven there was a knock on my door. I was hesitant about opening it because I was sure it wasn't Marnie or Jed appearing on my doorstep this early in the morning.

"Who is it?" I shouted.

"Detective Baldwin."

I sprang into action, quickly unlocked the door, and welcomed him into my home.

"Ms. Harris, you called about the photograph posted on the Internet?" he said both as a statement and a question.

"Yes sir, I did," I responded.

"I did see the photo before it completely disappeared. It didn't seem to be very clear. Are you sure that was your daughter Emily?" he asked.

"As far as I could tell, it looked like her; but like you said, it wasn't very clear," I said.

"Where was that photo taken?" he asked.

"I don't know, but I think it was taken inside the house in the woods at the end of this street," I answered.

"Who lives in that house?"

"It's empty and hasn't been lived in for years. At least, that is what I've been told. But—and this is a big but—I don't believe a word of it. Someone lives in that house and they are holding my daughter in there for whatever reason."

"Do you have any proof for that accusation?" Detective Baldwin demanded.

"No sir, I do not. It is just a gut feeling that has cropped up because she was interested in checking that place out. She wanted the snoop around and see what was inside the place," I answered back sternly.

"We can't arrest anyone on a gut feeling, and we certainly can't get a search warrant for a gut feeling. I must have some kind of proof," he said firmly.

"How am I supposed to get that proof if I can't get inside the place?" I asked.

"I'm sorry, ma'am, I don't have an answer to that question. Now, about that photograph. Are you sure that is your daughter? How long ago was it taken?" he asked.

"She was wearing those clothes when she disappeared, so it had to be taken about two days ago," I said as I started to fight back the tears of anger with Detective Baldwin's inaction and the fear of the danger that Emily might be facing.

I wiped at my eyes because I didn't want him to make any

conclusions because of the tears. I just wanted his help.

"Has she ever run away before?" he asked sternly.

Well—that was about all I could take from him and his accusation.

"She did not run away," I shouted loud enough to awaken my two children who were sleeping in separate bedrooms. "She sneaked out to meet a friend but she did not run away. There is a difference, you know. Didn't you ever sneak out of the house when you were a kid?" I demanded.

"What I did as a kid has nothing to do with this run away case, Ms. Harris. You are going to have to face the fact that your daughter may be a runaway who may never be found."

"Enough, Detective Baldwin. If all you can do is tell me that Emily is a runaway, I want you out of here. But before you go, can you tell me if you technical people were able to track down the website that transmitted the photo?" I demanded.

"No ma'am, they had not located it when I left to come here. I will ask them to continue to work on it, and I will get in touch with you if any new developments come up. In the meantime, I suggest you stay in touch with the friends and acquaintances of your daughter just in case she tries to speak with any of them," he suggested smugly.

He walked to the door and let himself out. I was afraid I would slam it behind him and shatter it to pieces. That was how angry I was feeling.

Both of my children stumbled into the living room rubbing their eyes trying to wake themselves up.

"Who was that?" asked Ellen.

"A detective who supposedly is looking for your sister."

"Supposedly?" asked Ryan.

"Yes, supposedly. He's not real interested in the search because he thinks she is a runaway. I'm sure he thinks looking for Emily should be someone else's job," I said sadly.

"What about Officer Whitt?" asked Ellen.

"Jed, Marnie, and I are going to meet her this afternoon at the house in the woods. At least she is still looking for Emily. She doesn't believe Em is a runaway," I explained.

"Good, someone believes us," said Ellen.

"When we go meet the officer, I need you two to stay here in case someone calls about Em, or maybe she calls to tell us where she is. Will you do that for me?" I asked my children.

"But we want to go with you," said Ryan.

"I really need you here," I said sternly. "Now, go get showered and dressed."

As soon as they left the room there was another knock on my door.

"Who is it?" I shouted.

"Jed, open up," he shouted back at me.

Chapter 21

When I opened the door for Jed, I saw Marnie park her car behind his. I offered coffee to the adults and poured myself a cup so we could get down to business.

"Please tell me you found out something about the photograph," I said as I turned my head from one to the other.

"Yes and no," said Jed as he heaved a big sigh. "I managed to print a copy off of the website before it disappeared, and I asked the technical people at the newspaper office to do what they could to find the origin. How about you, Marnie? Did you find anything?" asked Jed.

"No, not much. It was gone almost as soon as I found it. But like Jed, I asked the people I work with to see what they could find," Marnie answered.

"Wow, oh darn. I was hoping someone would find something," I said with disappointment.

"Have you checked it out this morning?" asked Jed. "I have my laptop right here. I'll enter her name again and see what pops up," he said with enthusiasm.

I hadn't checked the laptop because Ryan had it in his room and I hadn't wanted to disturb him when he was asleep.

"Is there anything new showing up?" I asked Jed.

"Yeah, there is another picture. It's different from the one you saw last night, isn't it?" he asked.

I looked over his shoulder and was shocked with what I was seeing before me.

"Look at her face," I said softly. "Someone has hit her and caused a bruise to appear. That is a bruise, isn't it?" I asked Jed.

"It looks like a bruise to me and look at the front of her shirt. That looks like a dark stain, maybe blood," he said softly.

"Oh my God, they have beaten my baby! Why have they hurt Emily?" I cried.

"Don't cry, Linds. We will find her, and she will be okay," said Marnie as she embraced me to offer me comfort.

"Can you tell anything about where that photo is coming from" I asked Jed.

"Yes, yes, I have an address here," he said as he rapidly copied it onto a piece of paper. "I'll call the people at work and see what they can find out."

"She looks okay, Linds. Maybe she is a little battered, but she is still alive. Be thankful for that, okay?" said Marnie.

"Let's go to the house in the woods to meet with Officer Whitt," I said as I glanced at the clock that was hanging on the wall next to the front door. "I know we will be early but we can do some checking on our own."

I told Ellen and Ryan that we were leaving and to let no one into the house unless they knew who was standing at the door.

Jed, Marnie, and I piled into one car and headed for the house in the woods.

We parked in the area in front of the trees. When we exited the car, we were each carrying flashlights and a weapon of sorts. Jed had a tire iron, I had a hammer, and Marnie carried something that looked like a croquet mallet except that it was much heavier than a wooden mallet.

We walked through the trees by following the path, and ap-

64

proached the porch with caution.

"Hold up, guys," I whispered. "Maybe we should walk all the way around the house before we try to go inside. I hadn't walked around to the back to see what was there, so I think maybe we should do that first."

"Yeah, that might be a good idea," said Jed. "We need to know what's waiting out behind this old house."

We stepped softly, watching every step we took to avoid making any kind of loud noise that would warn someone inside of our approach.

I was surprised at how large the three story house was on the outside. There were out buildings spread around behind the hulking house that you couldn't see from the front. My thought was that Emily could be anywhere in the house or one of the out buildings.

We walked around each out building looking inside through any windows we could find. We stood silently with our ears tuned to any sounds that might be emanating from the buildings.

Nothing.

We saw nothing.

We heard nothing.

We returned to scouting out the house. We walked as close to the house as we possibly could, ducking for cover in front of lower positioned windows. Then we would creep up to the windows to be able to sneak a peek to see what was inside that particular room.

The rooms were so dark, you could see nothing. That was strange because I would have thought some of the outside light would have filtered inside.

We tried to turn the knobs on each door we encountered, but none would allow us to enter.

We continued walking around the house until we were once again at the front porch.

"Marnie, this is your first time here. What do you think?" I asked as we stepped closer to the front door.

"Spooky, this place is really spooky," she whispered.

"Jed, do you think we should try to go inside now or wait until Officer Whitt arrives?" I asked.

"What time is it?" he asked.

"It's about noon or a little after. She should be here soon. She told me after lunch," I answered.

"Maybe we should wait," said Marnie.

"Okay, but let's go back to the car," I said as I started to lead the way.

"Wait, wait, Linds! I saw someone moving around inside. Look over there," he said excitedly as he pointed to the window on the left side of the front porch.

I ran over to the window and looked inside but I saw nothing.

"Where? I don't see anything," I said as I held my hands up to the sides of my head to shield my eyes from the sunlight.

A vision popped up in front of me filling the entire area of the window. I drew myself back and screamed.

"What is it?" asked Jed.

"I don't know. It was so sudden my brain couldn't catch it except that it told me to step back," I stammered.

"Was it a person?" asked Marnie.

"I think so, but I couldn't make out any characteristics other than that it was scary," I sputtered.

"Man or woman?" asked Jed.

"It was a thing. It could have been either," I said skeptically.

"Something or someone that big couldn't just disappear in a flash," said Marnie.

"Well—I guess it did," I said as my temper began to flare.

"I'm just saying it was some kind of a gimmick used to scare people away," she explained as she tried to calm me again.

"It's working. It seems to be scaring me away quite often," I

66

said with a grimace.

"Well, do you want to try to go in through the front door?" asked Jed.

"I'm game," I said. "I really want to know who is trying to scare me and why. I also want to know where Emily is being held. I'm sure she's in this house."

"Let's go," said Jed.

"I think we need to wait for Officer Whitt," said Marnie.

Chapter 22

We all congregated around Marnie's vehicle awaiting Officer Whitt's arrival.

My mind was, once again, reviewing horrible possibilities of torture and terror that Emily might be enduring. I was staring off in another world when Jed interrupted my thoughts.

"Linds, Linds, Earth calling Lindsay," Jed said as he jostled my shoulder, forcing me back into reality and away from the dreadful terror possibilities.

"What?" I snapped.

"Officer Whitt is coming," said Jed.

"Good," I whispered after I refocused my thoughts.

Officer Whitt was accompanied by a big, muscular, mountain of a man whom she introduced as Officer Williams. We all greeted each other with introductions to those who were new to the assemblage.

"What do you want us to do?" I asked.

"Just follow us for now," she said as she took in visually the small forest of trees. She was searching for sights that were out of the ordinary or different from her previous visit.

The path was large enough for us to travel two at a time without bumping into each other. The closer I walked toward the house, the more scared I became. I had just finished walking completely around the structure with Jed and Marnie and I didn't feel scared, or at least this scared, until the trip towards danger started again.

The fear was overtaking me to such a degree that I was shaking noticeably.

"Linds, are you okay?" asked Jed.

"Yes, I think so, but something bad is going to happen. I can feel it all the way to my soul."

"Nothing will happen. The cops are here to protect us," whispered Jed.

"Yeah, sure, right," I answered skeptically.

When we reached the front porch, the forward momentum came to a halt while Officer Whitt and Officer Williams made ready their weapons for use, if necessary.

That little movement of protection relieved my anxiety a bit but the thought 'how can you stop a ghost with a bullet?' raced through my mind causing a rise in fear, once again.

"You guys stay out here for a few moments. Officer Williams and I will go inside first to clear the entrance area," instructed Officer Whitt in a firm authoritative voice.

I didn't want to wait outside. I wanted to go crashing in so I could find my daughter. I consented to the wait, but paced around the front porch like a caged animal.

"Stop it," said Marnie. "You are making the rest of us nervous."

I stopped pacing, but I couldn't stop fidgeting.

This time when the police entered the house, there was no flash of light, no sudden darkness, and no loud threatening voices.

I inched myself closer and closer to the open front door where I could hear shouts of "clear" coming from two different voices.

"Can I come in?" I shouted from the front doorway.

"Yes," said a whispery voice that sounded nothing like Officer

Whitt or Officer Williams.

"Come on Jed, Marnie, we can go in now," I shouted to my two cohorts.

I was still apprehensive from my last attempt at entering this house. Marnie and Jed were almost pushing me inside when I hesitated at the door.

"Go on," whispered Jed. "We need to check this place out."

"Okay, okay," I replied with fear evident in my tone.

We walked further past the doorway into a foyer that was old and musty smelling. It really wasn't in as bad of a condition as I thought it might be. The wallpaper was still intact showing only signs the dust and dirt from no maintenance or cleaning, and it wasn't black as it had appeared previously.

"Keep going," said Marnie in a whisper that made her sound as scared as I felt.

I stepped through the foyer and into what looked like the main hall that was filled with a huge staircase and many closed doors leading to different rooms—a lot of different rooms. I stood there staring at the staircase that led both up and down. Up went to the second and third floors while down had to lead to the basement.

"Wow, what a place to live," whispered Jed as he spun around, taking in all the doors and staircase.

"Who could afford to build this house, let alone live in it?" asked Marnie.

"From what you've told me, no has lived in it. Isn't that right?" I said.

"Well, yes, that is what the court records say but why leave it vacant and unused for all of those years?"

"The murders caused that," I said.

"Do you think this place is haunted?" asked Marnie.

"Maybe," I replied as a cold chill raced down my spine.

"Sh-sh-sh," said Jed as he placed his index finger up to his lips.

We did as he suggested and heard nothing.

"I don't hear anything," I whispered.

"Yes, that's the problem," said Jed.

After a moment of pause, I realized what he was getting at. There were no walking, talking, any kind of movement sounds coming from the two people who had entered this establishment before us.

Marnie, who has not noticed the lack of noise said, "What's up?"

"Where did the cops disappear to?" asked Jed.

Marnie's mouth dropped open but no sounds came out. She had realized what the problem was, and had no answer.

"What should we do?" asked Marnie when her voice returned.

"We've got to keep searching. Emily has got to be here," I snapped.

Chapter 23

We stood in the center of the room that led to many different areas of the house. We each turned slowly looking, at all of the options.

"Should we go to three different rooms or stay together?" Marnie asked.

"Stay together," I said sternly. "We are much better off and more protected if we travel in a group."

"Pick a room," suggested Jed.

I chose the room on the right. That just seemed to be the natural choice since I am right handed.

We walked to the right where I turned the door knob. It was locked.

"Move, Linds, I'll open it," he said as he prepared to rush against the poor, defenseless door.

Bang.

The door flew open and hit the wall. We walked inside the room and saw what looked like the decorations for an old-fashioned parlor. Although it was dusty and musty, all of the furnishings were like new. There were crocheted doilies on the tables that had once upon a time been starched and sparkling white. There were cloth covered chairs and end tables in several places in the room. The wall paper was firmly adhering to wall and not hanging loose.

"Nothing in here looks out of place," I said as I turned to leave the room.

The next room was also to the right but a little closer to the staircase, and it was not locked. When we entered, we were shocked to see that it was completely ransacked. The chairs were turned over, the tables were knocked aside with some of them broken, and any item that was breakable was beyond repair.

"Why is this one wrecked?" Marnie asked in disbelief.

"I imagine it was because it was unlocked," I answered.

"That wouldn't matter to anyone who was out to do destruction. He would have smashed through the door just like I did," said Jed.

"Let's check out the other rooms on the first floor and then move up," I suggested,

"Have you heard any footsteps overhead?" asked Jed.

"No," I answered.

"I guess the cops aren't walking around over this room," said Jed.

"Maybe we should just go on up to the second floor and see what we can find there," I suggested.

"Let's do that," agreed Jed.

We clustered up and started climbing the huge staircase that not only led to the second floor, but actually continued up to a third floor.

"Second floor, let's check there first," I said and I glanced at the stairs rising to the third floor from the second floor landing.

There appeared to be four rooms on the second floor, because I saw only four doors. Of course, a door could lead to more than one room, but we wouldn't know that until we walked through one of those doors.

This time we turned left and stopped at the door to the room that was closest to us. It was locked and Jed did his smashing thing again. It looked like a room that had been lived in. There was a huge bed with linens that looked as if someone had been sleeping between the sheets.

I stepped closer to the bed and bent over so I could smell the sheets to help me determine if any human smell was recent. I got a whiff of sweat and body odor that had not had time to fade away.

"Someone been sleeping here recently," I whispered.

"How can you tell?" asked Jed.

"Take a sniff of the sheets. You can smell his presence in this room," I explained.

"Blood hound, are you?" asked Marnie.

"No, just a mother whose kids don't always want to change their sheets every week," I answered.

"The distinctive aroma makes me believe our sleeper may be a man," said Jed.

"Check out the room and see if you can find anything that is useful," I suggested

"And what is useful?" asked Marnie.

"Anything that might lead us to Emily," I snapped.

I looked under the bed, in the drawers of both chests, and checked the tiny little room that seemed to be a closet. I could find nothing that could be of any help to us.

"Now that we know there is someone living here, we need to find out who it is and why?" said Jed as he started to the door of the room. "We need to do some more checking and we need to find the cops and Emily."

"Okay," I said.

When we were outside of the room we had just checked, Jed stopped and listened again.

"Did you hear something?" I asked.

"Yes, but I don't know where it came from. It sounded so far away, which makes me think it is not on this floor. Let's go on up to the third floor before we go back downstairs. Perhaps the base-ment is the focal point of the search but we need to go topside first," Jed said solemnly.

We proceeded quietly, or as quietly as three people could be, on up to the third floor. We were surely surprised when we reached the top level, because it turned out to be one huge room possibly used for a ballroom. It was beautifully decorated with dusty pillars and exquisite wallpaper that glimmered in the sunlight filtering in through the many windows that were draped in velvet.

"Wow, could you imagine attending a dance in this place?" Marnie asked as she gazed at the surroundings.

"No, it's a shame that this place has been unoccupied or al-most unoccupied for so many years," I answered.

Obviously, there was nothing that would help us find those who were missing in the ballroom, so we returned to the staircase for the trip to the basement.

We weren't being quiet any longer. We trooped down the steps almost bouncing with each tread downward because we were going to find the truth, or so we thought.

The basement was where all of the musty smell emanated that filled the lower floors of the house. Of course, it was dark, and definitely uninviting, just as I knew it would be.

At the bottom of the steps of the huge staircase, we were standing on a landing that was surrounded by closed doors. It was not the picture of a normal basement where you would see bare wooden rafters, spider webs, and possibly dripping or run-ning water.

"Sh-sh-sh," said Jed as he tried to halt the exchange of words between Marnie and me.

"What now?" I asked curiously.

"Don't you hear that?" he whispered.

"No, what do you hear?" I asked.

"First it was a tapping and then a scratching."

"It's probably rats," I said with a grimace.

"A rat wouldn't dare set foot in this place," added Marnie.

"You're probably right about that, so let's see who or what is making the noise," said Jed.

"Which door to you want to smash?" I asked Jed with a smirk.

"Just a second. I want to listen outside of each of them so I can determine which one should be first," Jed said as he walked to the door directly in front of him and plastered his ear against it.

He continued on to the second, third, and fourth doors before he walked back to the first door and turned the doorknob.

The door opened, and he pushed it wide so we could all see inside. We each had flashlights at the ready and proceeded to follow him into the darkness. It was dark, too dark, even the walls appeared to be painted black.

I shined my flashlight around looking for a light switch. Then I realized that if I found a switch there was no electricity in the place.

We walked in a close group as we searched each of the walls for another ingress or egress. When we couldn't find anything, we moved on to the second door.

It was unlocked too, and was a spitting image of the room we had just checked out.

"Why would anyone want to paint the walls black?" I mumbled.

"Crazy people," responded Marnie. "This place gives me the creeps."

"Let's move on," said Jed as he led us to the third door.

It was locked.

"The fact that it is locked must mean something," I whispered to Jed and Marnie.

Bang.

Again, Jed smashed a door open and it crashed against the black wall. This room appeared to hold some of the necessary

76

equipment to maintain a household of this size. There were two water heaters and huge furnace, none of which were doing their specified jobs at the moment.

We quickly toured the room looking for doorways and passages, but could find nothing.

"Number four, coming up," said Jed. "I certainly hope we find something helpful in there."

Jed turned the doorknob of the fourth door but it did not open. He readied himself for the smash in, but that tough hit did not open the door.

"Guess this must be the place," muttered Jed as he rubbed his shoulder. "We are going to have to find something else to use on this door."

We all looked around and found nothing except for what we had been carrying as weapons. I grabbed the tire iron that Jed had been carrying and handed it to him.

"Use the tire iron. I have a hammer if you need it," I said in encouragement.

Jed struggled with shoving the sharp edge of the tire iron between the door and the frame next to the doorknob and locking apparatus.

"Hand me your hammer," he said as he held the tire iron in place.

He pounded on the tire iron with the hammer. The noise was loud and obvious. Someone was trying to break into the fourth room, and that someone was us.

The door banged open and, once again, we were in a black room.

"I'm getting real tired of this black paint being splashed on the walls everywhere," I mumbled as I looked inside the now open door.

We bunched up as close to each other as possible and entered the room that was behind door number four. Our steps were in unison, as was our breathing. We were all shaking with fear and probably would have died right there on the spot if we had heard a sudden sound.

Forward we scooted so Jed could see the walls more clearly. He stepped away from us and ran his hands over the blackness. He tapped lightly, listening for a difference in sounds. He moved to another wall and did the same maneuver with us close on his heels.

"I haven't found anything yet, but I'm sure there is something behind these walls," he whispered. "We need to move to the next wall."

He ran his hands over the black surface, feeling for cracks or openings that could not be seen in the darkness. He tapped in several different places and did the same thing again.

"I think there is something behind this wall."

"How do we get to it?" I asked excitedly.

"I don't know yet."

He ran his hands over the wall several more times until he stopped at what appeared to be a scratch on the black paint.

"It's here," he said as he grabbed the tire iron again and tried to shove it into the crack. After several noisy attempts, the tire iron went into the crack and Jed used the hammer, pounding on the tire iron until the hidden door gave way.

Inside we could see four people tied to chairs and squirming around as best they could to garner our attention.

"Emily!" I screamed as I ran toward my daughter.

Chapter 24

Jed had a pocket knife and that is what we used to remove all of the zip ties that held four people attached to chairs.

I stopped long enough to call my other children using my cell phone to let them know Emily was safe and on her way to the hospital for the once over by the doctors. We wanted to make sure there were no physical problems. The mental problems would take a much longer time to heal.

Tim Riley was picked up at the hospital by his aunt but not until the detectives questioned him relentlessly. They tried to do the same to Emily, but I put a stop to it by calling my boss, Wayne Maxwell, Attorney at Law, who intervened with the promise that I would take Emily to the police station the next day.

Officers Whitt and Williams were very embarrassed by the fact that they were both captured and held hostage by what appeared to be an old vagrant. All they were able to do was give a description to the authorities of the vagrant. They had no clue why all of this had happened.

Marnie, Jed, and I, piled into the car with Emily and drove to my house as three smiling adults. As soon as we got there, Marnie and Jed took off for their own homes and a breather from the fear and pressure we had all endured during the search for Emily, Tim, and the two police officers.

It never occurred to me that we might have more trouble awaiting us before the night was over. All I knew was that I was a happy mother with her family in tact once again.

"Emily, why did this happen?" I asked my daughter after she took a hot shower and dressed in her bed clothes.

"They were after Tim, I think. He seems to be the heir to some money that has been sitting unclaimed for many years," she answered.

"Who is the vagrant, the person who held you?" I asked.

"I don't know. He didn't talk much to me," she answered.

"Did he keep you guys separated some of the time?" I asked.

"Most of the time. When we were all together it was because he needed to keep a closer eye on us. Too many people had been trying to get into the house. He is the one who set up the flashes of light and the weird voices. The darkness was just natural."

"Why did they want Tim?"

"He is the one who will inherit the money. He and his brother, that is," said Emily.

"Where is Tim's brother?"

"I don't know; he said he had lost touch with him after they were split up when they were younger. Tim thinks he went into foster care, but he is not sure."

"Did you tell that to the police officers who were with you?" I asked.

"No, we didn't get to talk much because we weren't together and most of the time we were gagged."

"Oh my, are you sure you're okay?" I asked.

"Yes, Mom, I'm just glad to be home," she said as she hugged me close to her.

Ellen and Ryan emerged from their bedrooms, showered, and dressed in bedclothes.

Ellen ran to Emily, threw her arms around her, and said, "I

really missed you, Em. Please don't do that again."

Ryan repeated the same phrase as he hugged his sister.

"Good night, Em," said Ellen and Ryan as they turned to leave.

"One more thing, Em. Why did you sneak out to meet Tim?" I asked softly.

"He wanted me to help him find out who was living in his house. He knew the house was going to be his as soon as his brother was located. The legal authorities weren't sure if he was dead or alive but nothing was going to be done about the ownership of the house until they found out his status."

"He isn't your boyfriend?" I asked skeptically.

"No way! He is just a friend," Emily said with a smile.

"Good night, Em. We need to go talk to the police tomorrow. Get some sleep," I said as I walked to the living room.

I whispered a silent prayer of thanks for the safe return of my child.

Chapter 25

A knock at my door woke me from a sound sleep.

"Who is it?" I shouted angrily.

"Tim Riley. I need your help," he said with a voice cracking from tears.

I went to the front door and swung it open. "It's the middle of the night. Why do you need my help now?" I asked as I tried to hide my irritation.

"It's my aunt. I believe she had something to do with all of this."

"Why?"

"She kicked me out of the house. She said she was leaving town and wouldn't be back," he said sadly.

"I always knew she was a little strange, but this was not anything I expected."

"Where is she now?" I asked.

"I think she went to the house in the woods."

"Why?"

"She is looking for my brother," he said skeptically.

"Your brother? Is he the one who has been doing all of this?" I asked.

"I think so."

"Let me get the kids up so they can go with us. I don't think

82

I should leave them here alone with that vagrant running around loose. I'm also going to call Officer Whitt or at least ask them to forward a message to her. She needs to be involved in this."

Three groggy kids and Tim Riley climbed into my car for our excursion into the unknown. Once my brood found out what we were going to do, the sleepiness left each one of them.

I parked in the space on the street side of the trees and waited for a few moments to see if Officer Whitt would show up. I saw the blue flashing lights headed toward us and I breathed a sigh of relief. I would feel a lot more comfortable with a member of the police department with me.

"Officer Whitt, thanks for coming. Tim Riley says that he thinks that the vagrant is his missing brother and that his aunt is in cahoots with his brother to collect the full inheritance that should be split between the two brothers," I explained.

"That certainly makes sense. We need to find the brother before we can do anything more. He will be charged with kidnapping, 4 counts, among other miscellaneous charges that have not been written up yet," said Officer Whitt.

"I want to go with you," said Tim Riley as he climbed out of my car.

"That might not be a safe thing to do," said Officer Whitt.

"If he is my brother, I want to talk to him, especially since I know who he is. When he talked to me before, I didn't know he was my brother. He wouldn't tell me why he was doing any of this," said Tim.

"I want to go, too," I said. "I want to face down the man who stole my daughter. My kids will stay in the car with the doors closed and locked. Won't you?" I said as I looked at my children who were shaking their heads up and down in agreement.

"Okay, but the two of you have to stay behind me. Do you understand?" snapped Officer Whitt.

We crept through the small forest of trees and walked to the front porch. There was no sign of anyone moving around inside or outside the house.

"Where would he be hiding?" asked Officer Whitt.

"He sleeps on the second floor but he kept the four of you in the basement," I said. "As you know, the place is huge and he could be anywhere."

"We will start in the basement first and then work our way up," said the officer as she led us into the house.

We followed her without speaking a word. We kept our eyes wide open as we all carried flashlights to help us through this maze of a house.

We found nothing in the basement, for which I was truly grateful. I had had enough of that part of the house to last me a life time. Next, we scouted out the rooms on the first floor including some of the rooms I had not entered previously. The second floor was empty of humans other than the three of us, so we climbed to the third floor.

"He could be in any of the out buildings," I suggested. "Or, maybe he left town with Tim's aunt."

"No, I don't think she was able to get herself packed up and ready to go before we got here. She would have come here to pick him up," said Tim.

We reached the third floor and looked around for a few moments before we spotted what appeared to be a closet. When we looked at this floor previously, we hadn't notice the closet.

Officer Whitt walked to the closet and yanked the door open with her gun drawn and ready for use. I shined my flashlight into the closet as did Tim.

There was a sound of slight movement in a dark corner. We aimed our flashlights at the sound and saw the vagrant huddling inside with his arms wrapped around himself.

"Thomas?" said Tim.

There was no response.

"Thomas?" said Tim, again.

The vagrant moved his head around to look at Tim. The bright light from the flashlight did not allow him to see Tim clearly.

"Go away!" the vagrant shouted.

"Thomas, come out of there," said Tim in a strong, demanding voice.

"Put your hands up!" shouted Officer Whitt.

Thomas raised his hands to the air and walked out of the closet.

He was dressed in rags consisting of two torn tee shirts and a pair of holey jeans that were not the stylish sort. His shoes were well worn, possibly white tennis shoes, and he had a dirty bandana tied over his dirty, stringy brown hair.

"Thomas, why are you living like this?" Tim asked.

"I ran away from that house I was living in. I didn't like those people," he mumbled.

"Did they mistreat you?" Officer Whitt asked.

"Not so much, I just didn't like all the rules," he sputtered.

"You are under arrest Thomas Riley," said Officer Whitt as she placed handcuffs on his emaciated wrists.

"Can I have something to eat?" asked Thomas.

"Sure, when we get to the police department," said Officer Whitt. "You can also get cleaned up so we can see how much you look like your brother."

"What's going to happen now?" asked Tim.

"He will need a good lawyer, and he will likely go to prison. He really could use the help and support of his long-lost brother, don't you think?" said Officer Whitt.

We all left the house in the woods and returned to our normal lives.

When I went to work the next day, I asked Wayne to help Thomas. I let Jed and Marnie know about everything they had missed after they left for their respective homes.

In a family conference, we all decided that haunted houses or anything related to strange houses can become a real problem and that snooping can be scary!

ABOUT THE AUTHOR

Linda Hudson Hoagland of Tazewell, Virginia, a graduate of Southwest Virginia Community College, has won acclaim for many of her novels: *Snooping Can Be Uncomfortable, Snooping Can Be Helpful–Sometimes, Onward & Upward, Missing Sammy, Snooping Can Be Doggone Deadly, Snooping Can Be Devious, Snooping Can Be Contagious, Snooping Can Be Dangerous*, and *The Best Darn Secret*, that are published by Jan-Carol Publishing Inc.

Hoagland has also written other fiction, nonfiction, poetry, and short stories that have been included in many anthologies including *Broken Petals, Easter Lilies, These Haunted Hills*, and *Wild Daises* that are published by Jan-Carol Publishing, Inc.

Hoagland is a retired Tazewell County School System employee, where she worked as a Purchase Order Clerk for almost 23 years. She is the proud mother of two sons.

Visit her website: www.lindasbooksandangels.com.

MEMBERSHIPS/ AFFILIATIONS

Member, Bluefield State College Humanities Degree Program Advisory Board, Bluefield WV

Member, Tazewell County Habitat for Humanity Board

Member, Planning Committee, Appalachian Heritage Writers Symposium

Member, Poetry Society of Virginia

Member, The Writers Workshop of Asheville, NC

Member, Virginia Writers Club, Somerset VA

Member, Appalachian Authors Guild, Abingdon VA, Past President and Vice President

Member, Lost State Writers Guild, TN & VA

Member, Writers-Editors Network, North Stratford NH

Member, Green River Writers, KY

Member, Lead Program, Richlands VA

Member, Friends of the Library Tazewell County

COMING SOON

In keeping with the events of today, Lindsay, family, and friends, managed to get involved with the world of drugs when they are unfortunately pulled into that world while trying to help a school mate of Ryan, her eleven year old son. They soon discover that *SNOOPING CAN BE REGRETTABLE.*

LINDSAY HARRIS MURDER MYSTERY SERIES

BY LINDA HUDSON HOAGLAND

JAN-CAROL PUBLISHING, INC

Linda Hudson Hoagland has authored and published many books, including poetry, and is an accomplished writer. She has received recognition and numerous awards throughout her writing career.

WWW.LINDASBOOKSANDANGELS.COM

www.ingramcontent.com/pod-product-compliance
Lightning Source LLC
Chambersburg PA
CBHW031855170626
46807CB00004B/1735